JUST DISGUSTING!
ANDY GRIFFITHS

with illustrations by
TERRY DENTON

PAN

Pan Macmillan Australia

The characters and events in this book are fictitious and any resemblance to real persons, living or dead, is purely coincidental.

First published 2002 in Pan by Pan Macmillan Australia Pty Limited
St Martins Tower, 31 Market Street, Sydney

National Library of Australia
Cataloguing-in-Publication data:

Griffiths, Andy, 1961– .
Just disgusting.

For children and teenagers.
ISBN 0 330 36368 9.

I. Denton, Terry, 1950– . II. Title.

A823.3

Designed and typeset in 12/16pt New Aster by Liz Seymour
Printed in Australia by McPherson's Printing Group

Contents

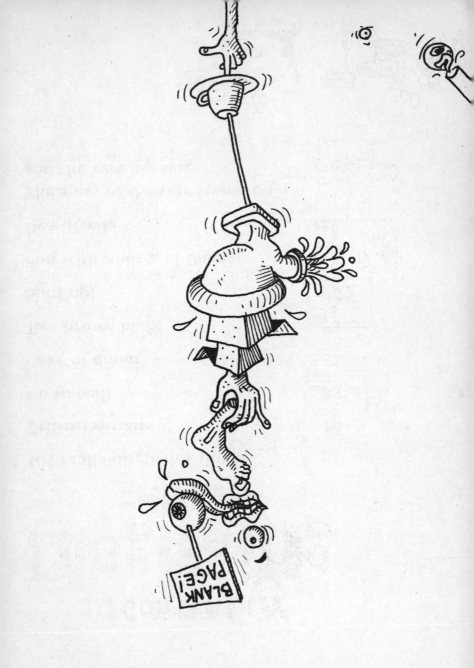

101 REALLY
Disgusting
THINGS

1. Brussel sprouts.

2. Maggots.

3. Brussel sprouts with maggots in them.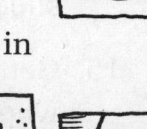

4. Picking your nose.

5. Picking your nose and eating it.

6. Picking somebody else's nose and eating it.

7. Scabs.

8. Scabs with maggots.

9. Maggots with scabs.